With warm purrs

& soft meows from "Big Red" & me.

Brian Heinz

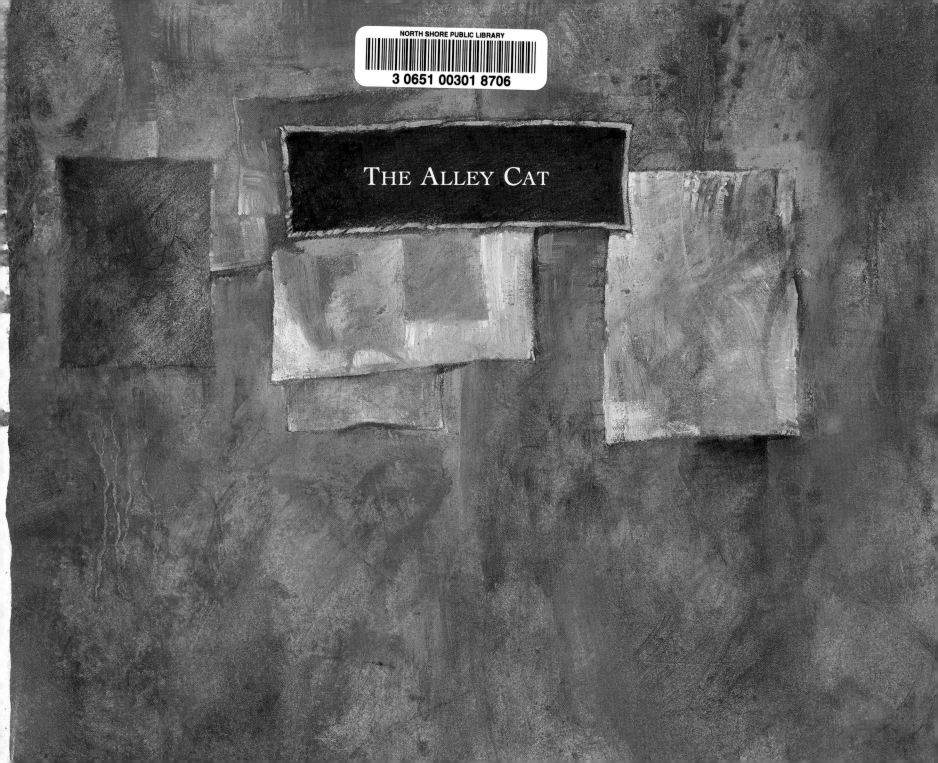

THE ALLEY CAT

A Doubleday Book for Young Readers

THE ALLEY CAT

by Brian J. Heinz

Illustrated by

David Christiana

A Doubleday Book for Young Readers

Published by
Delacorte Press
Bantam Doubleday Dell Publishing Group, Inc.
1540 Broadway
New York, New York 10036

Doubleday and the portrayal of an anchor with a dolphin
are trademarks of Bantam Doubleday Dell Publishing
Group, Inc.

Copyright © 1993 by Brian J. Heinz
Illustrations copyright © 1993 by David Christiana
Type design by Carol Malcolm-Russo

Library of Congress Cataloging-in-Publication Data

Heinz, Brian J.
    The alley cat / Brian J. Heinz ; illustrated by David
Christiana.
        p. cm.
    Summary: A scarred and tattered alley cat ventures
into the dangerous world of the city at night to find food
for his mate and little ones.
    ISBN 0-385-31042-0
    [1. Cats—Fiction.   2. Stories in rhyme.]
I. Christiana, David, ill.   II. Title.
PZ8.3.H41344A1   1993
[E]—dc20   91-47135
                                                         CIP
                                                          AC

RL: 2.6
Manufactured in Hong Kong
June 1993
10 9 8 7 6 5 4 3 2 1

For Bijou and her cat, Marcellou

—B.J.H.

Thanks Harley and Skeeto

. . . and Flower, too

—D.C.

Seething, steaming sewer grates,
Heaps of rotted packing crates.

Subways grumble deep beneath
The potholes on the city street.

Arching backs and stretching limbs
Are framed in shadows. Night begins.

Grimy drizzle coats the street
To wet and blacken padded feet.

Beyond the alley, headlights shine.
Beyond the alley, sirens whine . . .

In the world of Alley Cats.

Our hero stands in stockinged feet
With preened red fur and snaggled teeth.

His ears are tattered, torn, and scarred,
His muscles tense, and lean, and hard.

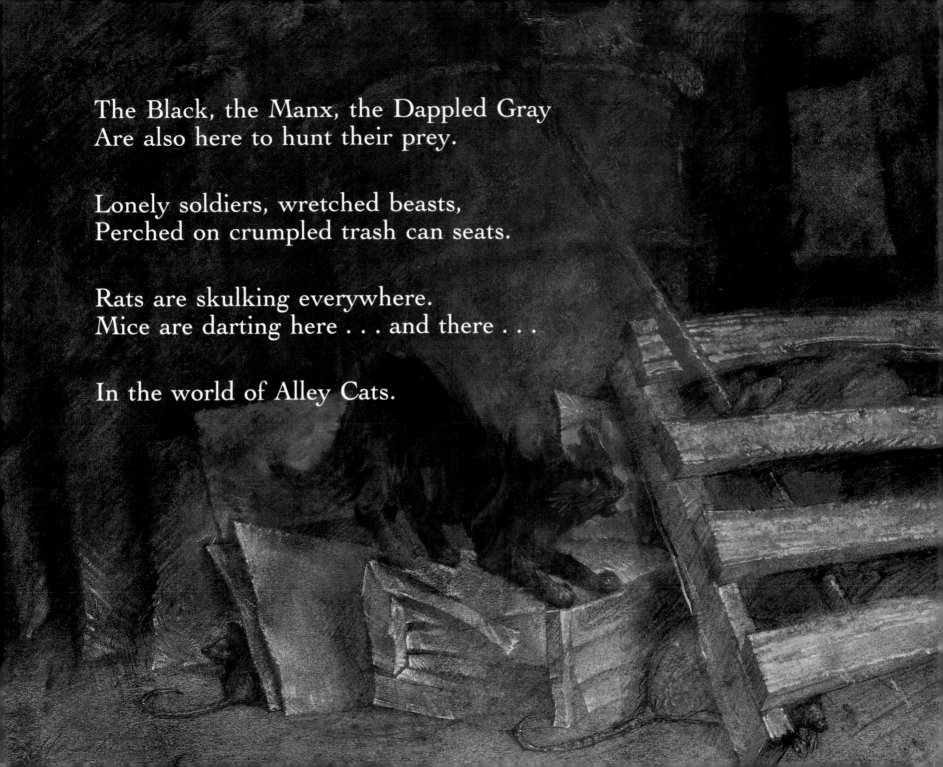

The Black, the Manx, the Dappled Gray
Are also here to hunt their prey.

Lonely soldiers, wretched beasts,
Perched on crumpled trash can seats.

Rats are skulking everywhere.
Mice are darting here . . . and there . . .

In the world of Alley Cats.

An iron door groans in the night
And throws out shafts of blinding light

That cut the alley like a knife.
It must be . . . Yes! The butcher's wife.

A monstrous woman thick of brow
With shoulders broader than a cow,

She squints through cold, unfeeling eyes.
Her thick hands heave the tasty prize.

She's gone. The pork chop strikes the ground
And all is still. There's not a sound . . .

In the world of Alley Cats.

The Calico stares in deadly silence.
Big Red is up and poised for violence.

They crouch. They stalk. They circle round
As bellies brush across the ground.

Our hero lunges at his foe!
He strikes! And whirls upon his toe.

In tangled turns they rip out hair
Like furry corkscrews in the air.

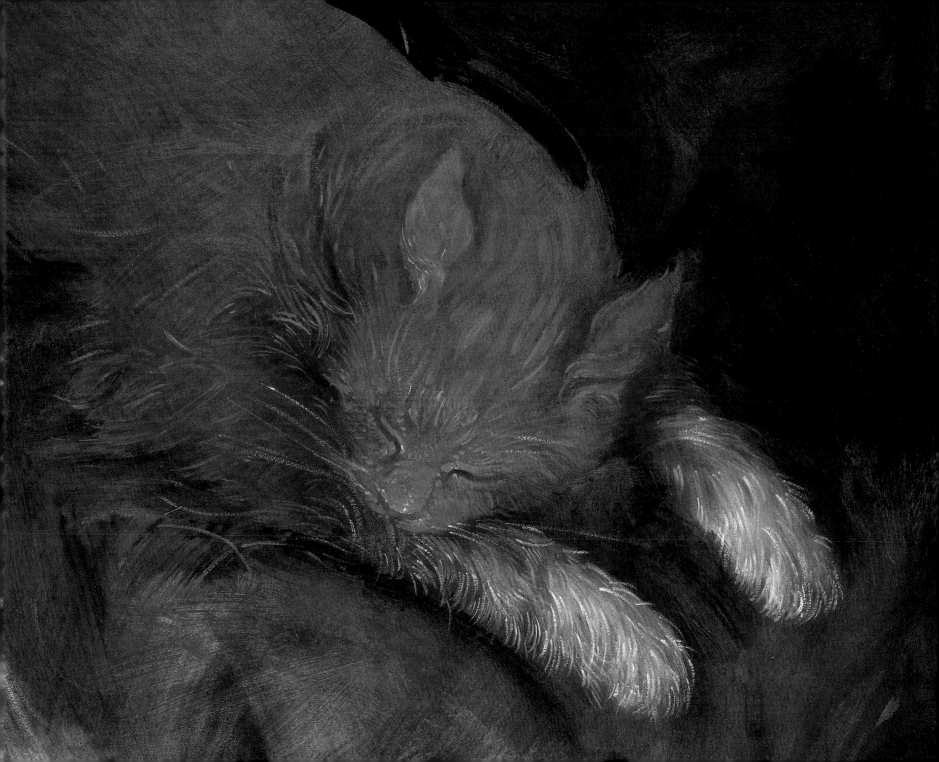

They writhe and roll, and skip and skittle,
Hiss and spit, and bleed . . . a little,

In the world of Alley Cats.

Calico has failed the test,
A limping, sore, bedraggled mess.

They might be friends tomorrow night,
But meat is scarce. They had to fight.

The audience now steals away,
The Black, the Manx, the Dappled Gray.

The hero proudly claims his prize
And struts about with glowing eyes.

Moonbeams drifting into town
Light Red's path. He's homeward bound!

In the world of Alley Cats.

He races under warehouse eaves,
A whirlwind kicking scattered leaves.

Painted scrawls across the wall
Of broken bricks about to fall—

And there! The broken window pane . . .
He leaps—and he is home again.

Outside? Danger fills the air.
Outside? Yes, life's quite unfair.

But in this dim and musty place
Red sees a soft, familiar face.

In the world of Alley Cats.

No claws . . . no fangs . . . no need for fear,
His little ones and mate live here.

The Tabby licks his matted hair.
She nuzzles him with loving care.

He purrs and curls up close beside her.
His heart is glad, this brave provider.

Here's his pack of mewling kittens
Dressed in stripes and small white mittens.

He cuffs them gently, one by one,
Three lovely girls and two fine sons.

Beyond gray walls, the night winds moan.
They're not afraid. They're not alone . . .

In the world of Alley Cats.